ING POLICY:
U D.' AGE OR LOSE LIBRARY MATERIALS,
WIL   FOR REPLACEMENT.
              MAR 31   APR 8 2006   PRIVILEGES,
ES, T. ANSC.   DIPLOMAS, AND REGISTRATION
ILEGES OR ANY COMBINATION THEREOF.
    MAR 2 '98
    MAR 22 '9
    MAY 20 '9

TWO KINDS OF PATRIOTS

Two Kinds of Patriots

LUCY JANE BLEDSOE

FEARON EDUCATION
a division of
David S. Lake Publishers
Belmont, California

Cover illustrator: Jim Pearson

ISBN 0-8224-4753-3

Library of Congress Catalog Card Number: 88-81522

Printed in the United States of America

1. 9 8 7 6 5 4 3 2 1

FAMILY TREE

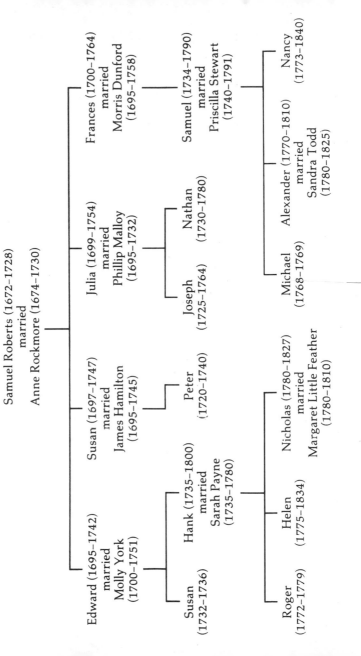

Samuel Roberts (1672–1728)
married
Anne Rockmore (1674–1730)

Edward (1695–1742)
married
Molly York
(1700–1751)

Susan (1697–1747)
married
James Hamilton
(1695–1745)

Julia (1699–1754)
married
Phillip Malloy
(1695–1732)

Frances (1700–1764)
married
Morris Dunford
(1695–1758)

Samuel (1734–1790)
married
Priscilla Stewart
(1740–1791)

Hank (1735–1800)
married
Sarah Payne
(1735–1780)

Peter
(1720–1740)

Joseph
(1725–1764)

Nathan
(1730–1780)

Susan
(1732–1736)

Roger
(1772–1779)

Helen
(1775–1834)

Nicholas (1780–1827)
married
Margaret Little Feather
(1780–1810)

Michael
(1768–1769)

Alexander (1770–1810)
married
Sandra Todd
(1780–1825)

Nancy
(1773–1840)

AN AMERICAN FAMILY™ SERIES

Contents

TWO KINDS OF PATRIOTS

A Rebellion in the Making

"Tarnation!" growled Private Hank Roberts. He picked up a piece of dirt from the cabin floor. Then he threw it at the small bag of wheat flour next to the fireplace. A rat slowly waddled away from the flour.

Hank reached for another piece of dirt. He threw this one at the man who sat sleeping in front of the smoking embers.

"Dorian, you fool," Hank muttered. "Can't we trust you for a two-hour watch? First you let the fire die. And then you let rats eat our rations." The dirt bounced off Dorian. But the big, rough-looking man didn't stir.

Hank fell back on the hard bed made of lashed-together poles. Like most of the men in the Continental Army, he had been a farmer. He'd made it through many hardships in his lifetime. But this winter of 1777 and 1778, camping at Valley Forge, was the toughest period of his life.

Hank Roberts was 43 years old. He had shaggy, light brown hair, and deep brown eyes. Since their corporal died of camp fever, most men in Hank's squad of Pennsylvania Militiamen turned to him for leadership.

Hank gritted his teeth and pushed himself up in bed. In September, he had been shot in the leg during the battle at Brandywine. The lead bullet was still sunk in Hank's leg. It pained him more than he could bear at times.

Still, Hank was glad he wasn't forced to stay in the camp hospital. The place was just an old barn. Once a man was taken there, it seemed he faced certain death. At night the wind carried the screams and moans from the hospital all the way across the camp. No, Hank had no need for doctors or hospitals.

Hank had taken care of the wound himself. But he knew he was lucky, too. He'd seen many a wounded leg go dead with gangrene. The limb would turn green, then black. Finally it would fall off like a leaf dropping from a tree.

Fortunately for Hank, his flesh grew right around the bullet. The wound left him with a limp and a lot of pain. But at least he was alive. And he had both of his legs and arms.

Many men in the Continental Army were not so lucky. Two thousand had died at the Brandywine battle in September. Even more had died at the Georgetown battle. Finally in December, General Washington's entire Continental Army—11,000 troops—had moved to this camp at Valley Forge.

Now, in February, only 9,000 men were left. A few had deserted. A few more had starved. But most were killed off by camp fever. Hank spent a part of each day digging graves in the hard frozen ground. Usually, to save strength, the soldiers dumped many bodies in each grave. They'd even given up covering over these death pits. Why bother? Tomorrow there would be more.

Sleep for Hank was nearly impossible. The aching hunger in his stomach and the pain in his leg kept him awake most nights. Now he sat in bed just before dawn trying to keep warm. Suddenly he heard the door to the cabin crack open. A piercing wind ripped through the crack. Snow swept in before Ike, a 16-year-old Oneida Indian boy, could close the door behind him.

"Shut the door," roared Dorian, suddenly awake. He was the kind of person who hated anyone he didn't understand. Ike certainly fit that description.

Several of the other men awoke, groaning from the cold, their hunger, and their wounds. Hank, coughing, limped to the fireplace. The smoke got so thick in the cabins that some of the men preferred to have no fire. But of course then they might freeze to death. Hank stoked the fire.

"What's the kid got there?" asked Dorian, rubbing his eyes.

Hank figured Ike had been outside to relieve himself. But now he saw the boy was holding two rabbits by the ears. In his other hand he held his bow and arrow.

Dorian jumped from the fireside. "Give me those rabbits, boy!"

Ike was small, but he never blinked in the faces of men like Dorian. His tribe, the Oneida, was one of two Iroquois tribes to join the colonists in the War for Independence. Though most Oneida were part of Captain Allan McClain's Oneida Scouts, Ike chose to join the Pennsylvania Militiamen.

He was a handsome boy with long black hair. His real name wasn't Ike of course. But "Ike" was as close as the men in the squad could come to pronouncing his real name. Ike didn't seem to mind. He was smart and had a good sense of humor. Hank thought he was one of the more mature soldiers in their squad.

As Dorian lunged at the boy, Ike yanked the rabbits behind his back. Dorian snatched the young Indian by his buckskin jacket. He began to shake the boy, hard. Dorian yelled, "Why should you eat when a white man is starving?"

"Because he knows how to catch rabbit in the winter," Hank answered. "Let go of the boy."

"Oh, I'll bet he caught them!" Dorian sneered. "Did you hear the fire of a musket? I ain't heard a sound this morning. The boy *stole* these rabbits. Give them here, or I'll report you to Captain Alexander for stealing."

"You better give them over," said Dorian's pal, a big man named Ronald. Both Dorian and Ronald were from Philadelphia. Hank didn't like them. He figured city boys expected everything to be easy. "You better give them to him," Ronald said again.

"Leave him alone," said a farmer named Wallace. Hank and Wallace pulled Dorian off Ike.

"You didn't hear musket fire because he used his bow and arrow," Wallace said.

"What kind of fool are you?" Hank asked Dorian. "Ike caught these rabbits. He could have built a fire and eaten them in the woods.

Instead, he was generous enough to bring them back to the cabin. Now we got two choices. We can shut up, cook the rabbits, and eat them. Or you can keep making a scene and draw the rest of the camp in here. Think of how big a bite you'll get when these rabbits are split among 9,000 men."

Dorian backed off. But Hank was scared by the anger burning in the big man's eyes. As if hunger, cold, and camp fever weren't bad enough. Every day it seemed that more and more men were at each other's throats. Just yesterday Hank saw two men fighting like wild cats over a small ragged hat. Something had to be done. Soon.

Hank spoke quietly to Ike as the boy skinned the rabbits. "You know you could have gotten shot for leaving quarters without permission."

The boy nodded.

"Why'd you do it?"

"I was hungry."

Hank nodded. It really was that simple. Though he was just sixteen, Ike managed better than many of the men. Ike said that

Indians were used to long periods of fasting. He had known hunger before. He didn't doubt that he would survive. Besides winter hunting, Ike knew other useful things. He taught Hank that it was a good idea to rub warmed beeswax on his feet. This helped keep out the cold and prevented chilblains.

While Ike worked on the rabbits, Hank mixed some wheat flour and water for firecakes. He put the patties on hot stones. Often the men were so hungry they ate their rations half-cooked. This morning they waited for the rabbits to cook. Two rabbits split among twelve men meant only a few mouthfuls each. Yet, compared to most days when they ate only firecakes, this was a feast.

"If it weren't for Washington, we'd be eating good everyday," Dorian said wiping his mouth.

"I sure think General Gates could do a better job," Ronald said. He always backed up Dorian.

"The writing is on the wall," Dorian went on. "Two thousand men died at Brandywine, led by General Washington. At Saratoga, General Gates led the Continental Army to victory. What could make it clearer that Washington doesn't know what he's doing?"

"We've lost so many battles, I don't even know what victory feels like," Wallace said.

"There's a meeting tomorrow night," Ronald said quietly. "You heard about it?"

"Shut up," Dorian snarled.

"Don't be foolish," Hank agreed. It was a bad idea to go around openly talking about mutiny. There were spies everywhere.

Hank knew a group of men were trying to stage a rebellion. In a way, he didn't blame them. There sure wasn't any glory in rotting, starving, or freezing to death. But a rebellion would just mean more bloodshed.

"Come on Ike," Hank said, getting two pails and limping to the door. "Let's go get the water."

Outside they walked toward the river in the cold morning light. In the distance Hank saw the commanding officer of his company, Captain Alexander. The tall, stately man always wore knee-high boots. Even from far away Hank could hear his deep booming voice. The captain liked to speak of the American cause like a preacher—often, and at great length.

"Look," Hank said, pointing. "There's Captain Alexander. And I believe that's General Washington with him." Hank stopped to stare. He'd never seen Commander-in-Chief George Washington before. High-ranking officers did not mix with privates.

Hank noticed that Ike didn't answer, or even look at the officers. So Hank said, "The captain certainly supports Washington. I've heard him speak very strongly about American independence."

"He's loud, anyway," Ike said. Hank was surprised. Captain Alexander was admired by nearly everyone in camp. The boy continued, "I think there are two kinds of patriots. The men of big words, and the men of action."

Hank nodded. There was a lot of sense in that. When they arrived at the river, Hank dipped the buckets in the icy water. He filled both and handed one to Ike.

Walking back up the hill, Ike asked, "Do you really think there will be a soldier uprising?"

"Look around," Hank said. "A third of the men are stewing in sweaty fever. At least half have no shoes or shirts. Almost no one has a jacket or a blanket."

Ike nodded. "Yet these men find the strength to fight each other for an extra firecake."

Hank stopped to tighten the rags wrapped around his feet. "Yes. A rebellion would just be doing the redcoats a favor. We would kill ourselves off and save them the trouble."

Hank shook his head sadly. He hated war. No matter what you did in war, it seemed to be wrong. There were no winners in war. Everyone got hurt.

At first, when the war began, he had agreed with the Loyalists. He believed the colonists ought to make changes through legal means. Petitions, letters, that sort of thing. The hotheaded, loudmouthed patriots had angered him. No good could come from killing, he thought.

"Oh, they like to hear themselves talk," he had told his wife Sarah. And he still believed many of the patriots were fonder of war itself than of independence.

But then came that unforgettable day last summer. In a few short hours, Hank completely changed his mind about the War of Independence. He shook with anger each time he thought of that day. And he'd remember what happened for as long as he lived.

Raid
of the Redcoats

Hank Roberts had been living happily with his wife Sarah and their two children. They owned a farm on the Schuylkill River not far from Philadelphia.

Hank had had a falling out with his father who was a shoemaker. So he never learned the trade or inherited his father's business. But Hank couldn't complain. He didn't want to work under his father's critical eye, anyway. So he became a farmer.

The previous summer, when the Declaration of Independence was signed, Hank became worried. He knew the British took advantage of the colonists. And he certainly believed that independence was a good idea.

But he wasn't sure that simply declaring the colonies free was the best course of action.

Hank knew that the British would use force to tighten their grip on the colonies. And he felt sure that a war would bring only bad things to his family. But he certainly never dreamed of going off to fight.

Until that hot August day.

Hank had just finished harvesting a fine wheat crop. Most years he raised little more than the family needed. But this year there was extra. Sarah and his daughter could have new dresses. His son would get his first suit. They would all get new shoes.

Even Sarah's vegetable crop was plentiful that year. In fact, he and Sarah were standing among the squash when Hank first spied the redcoats.

Hank wasn't alarmed at first. The British were a common sight in the region. The Swede who owned the neighboring farm had already been visited by them.

"You wouldn't believe the gold," bragged the man. "Falling out of their pockets like a farmer's dirt!" The Swede showed Hank and Sarah the gold he'd been given in exchange for his crops. It looked to be several hundred dollars worth of coins.

"What will you eat?" asked Sarah.

"With gold like this, who needs to eat?" laughed the farmer. Then he advised, "Put a little food aside. Sell the rest to the British. You'll be rich like me!"

Hank wasn't convinced. However he felt about the patriots, he wouldn't support the redcoats. And when a group of five British soldiers rode up that afternoon, he was prepared to tell them this.

"Can I help you?" Hank asked in a friendly manner.

"In the name of the king, we've come to buy your wheat and produce," the man in charge announced.

"I'm afraid I've none extra, men. Good day." Hank took Sarah's hand and began to walk toward the house. The five soldiers jumped down from their horses and followed them.

Hank turned. "I'll have to ask you to leave. I have nothing to sell."

The man in charge wore a stiff smile. He reached in his pocket and pulled out a small sack. Then he took Hank's hand and placed the sack in it. "Gold," he said. "Does that change your mind?"

Hank shoved the sack of gold back at the soldier. "I warn you," Hank said. "I will not be bought. Now I order you off my land immediately."

The soldier, still wearing his stiff smile, stepped toward Sarah. He put an arm around her shoulder and drew her to him. "The lady likes gold, I bet."

"Let go," Sarah cried, trying to pull herself free. But the man only held her tighter.

"You'll sell, now, won't you?"

"You're animals," Hank growled. He tried to pull the soldier away from Sarah. In an instant, four muskets were shoved into his ribs.

The man holding Sarah let her go. "He's a touchy one, isn't he?" he said to his men.

Then to Hank he added, "You won't sell. Then we will have to take. You and the woman, *march*."

Hank and Sarah were marched into their own kitchen at gunpoint. "I need to get my children," Sarah announced.

The soldiers let her go upstairs to get the children, who were napping. Then the family sat in the kitchen huddled together while one soldier held a gun on them. The other soldiers then searched the entire house for things to take.

Armloads of clothes were carried downstairs and out to waiting wagons. The men picked Sarah's vegetables and took Hank's tools. They loaded up the sacks of wheat flour from the Roberts's barn. They slaughtered four cows and one pig on the spot. Finally, one soldier came down the stairs carrying Sarah's only two pieces of jewelry. One piece Hank had given her when they married. The other had belonged to Sarah's mother.

"Oh, no you don't!" Hank jumped up.

A bayonet jabbed him in the stomach. "Do not interfere," the soldier warned him. Then he took his bayonet to the curtains and tore them just for fun.

By the time the soldiers left, they had carried off the entire summer harvest. And they had wrecked the house, destroying nearly everything the family owned.

Even so, if that had been the end of it, perhaps Hank and Sarah could have gone on. They might have planted for an autumn harvest. They could have gotten by somehow. But Hank knew that their house was marked. The redcoats would keep coming back for anything they grew—or just to torture them.

Holding their children, Hank and Sarah sat in silence for a long time. Finally Hank said, "I'm going to sign up. You can go live with my sister in Stonesbury, Massachusetts. At least in the Continental Army I shall be able to draw a salary and send you and the children money."

"I guess there is little choice," Sarah whispered.

So it was decided. Out of anger and necessity, Hank would do what he never thought he would—go to war.

That night he and Sarah stayed up late trying to comfort one another. Hank thought that surely this was the worst moment he'd ever have in his life. How was he to know that the nightmare had just begun?

The Meeting in the Woods

The night of the mutiny meeting, Hank lay awake in bed. He thought about his family. Several months ago the privates' pay of $6.67 a month had been cut off. Since then he had had nothing to send to them. But at least they were safe with his sister and her husband. He knew they had a roof over their heads and food on the table.

Hank heard the men sneaking out of the cabin, one by one. A man caught leaving camp at night could be shot. But Hank had heard that the men on watch tonight were in on the rebellion plan.

After each man left, Hank silently counted to 100. He figured it would take that long for the men to reach the edge of the woods. He heard no gunshots.

Then Hank heard Ike get up.

"Where are you going?" Hank whispered angrily. He felt he needed to protect the boy.

"I have to know what's going on," Ike said. "I'm going to listen."

"You could get shot."

Ike gave a short laugh. "Why shoot the few of us that are strong enough to move?"

Hank rolled off his bed of poles, rubbing his bad leg. "Wait, I'll go with you."

A light snow was falling. Ike had on a fairly warm buckskin jacket. But Hank had only a wool shirt that was more holes than cloth. At least the cold numbed the pain in his leg.

Nearby two sentries warmed their hands over a tiny fire. Hank stopped, putting a hand on Ike's arm. Surely the sentries heard the crunch of feet in the snow. But the men kept their backs turned. They acted as if they did not hear or see a thing.

Hank and Ike slipped into the black forest on the edge of camp. They walked as softly as they could, pushing through the ice-coated underbrush. Soon Hank saw a shimmering glow on the trees. They arrived at the blaze the men had built.

Hank looked around at the group of several dozen soldiers. Men from all parts of the country were there. A howling wind whipped through the trees, but Dorian's voice rose above it.

"General Howe and the British are in Philadelphia. They're sitting only 20 miles away, watching us freeze and starve to death. They don't need to march a step. They don't have to fire a single musket. And why should they, when our own general lets us die like dogs?"

"I think General Washington wants to prove we're not frightened," said Wallace.

"What a joke! I hear that Howe and his men are having one long party this winter in Philadelphia." Dorian shot back an answer at every chance.

"Well, that's not Washington's fault," Wallace replied. "It's those rotten Loyalists who are feeding and housing them! I see Washington's point about sticking close to the enemy because—"

"I don't see *anyone's* point without my pay," said a southerner named Parker. "We haven't seen our $6.67 in months."

"Wouldn't matter if we did see it," Ronald put in. "Continental money is worthless."

"Forget money," cried Williams, a black man. "I want food and clothes—now. Heck, I was sent to take the place of my master. He promised me freedom for serving his time. But I want to know what good freedom is to a *dead* man? I haven't had a decent meal in weeks."

"Yeah, well, I happen to be from Virginia, like Washington," another soldier said. "And there isn't a richer man in the colonies." He has land, slaves, finery like you've never seen. He doesn't know what hunger or cold means."

"Look, don't you think Washington wants to feed, dress, and pay us?" Hank asked. "The problem is those boys in Congress. They're too busy writing their documents to think about the soldiers doing the *fighting*. I heard Washington's been writing them letters everyday asking for food and clothes. They ignore him."

Wallace said, "Those documents don't hold any weight if we're not fighting."

"Right," said Hank. "But fighting each other, or fighting General Washington, can't help anyone."

"If you're so sure about Washington, what are you doing here?" Dorian said. He pushed aside a man to get closer to Hank. "You some kind of spy?"

"I'm here because maybe we can work out something, come up with a better plan for finding food. We could send out parties to local farmers—"

"It's been done. They're not going to take worthless Continental dollars when they can get gold from the redcoats."

"Well, we should hunt more—"

"Who's got the strength? There's not much game out there anyway. It's February, remember?"

Hank knew these were poor solutions. But there had to be something they could do to hold on until spring.

"I say rebel," Dorian cried. "Let's show Washington a thing or two. I'm not staying here just to starve to death."

"Quiet," Ike said, throwing a hand in the air. His eyes sparked with danger. "Someone's coming."

But it was too late. With the deep snow, the crackling fire, and Dorian's loud voice, no one had heard the horse and rider approach. The man pulled his horse into the ring of campfire light. Hank and the other men could only stare.

The first thing anyone noticed was that the stranger looked well fed and warmly dressed. He was tall, blond, and he sat straight on his horse. He seemed quite sure of himself even before he spoke. A conceited smile spread across his lips.

"Well!" he announced with a strong southern drawl. "Isn't this a fine sight. A group of soldiers planning who knows what in the wee hours of the morning! I am at Valley Forge, am I not?" He looked around, but no one moved or spoke.

"Perhaps I would get an answer if I added that I'm a new corporal reporting to Captain Alexander."

A few men struggled to their feet and saluted. Hank, angered by the man's conceit, remained seated. The new corporal addressed him. "You, Private. Perhaps you can tell me the purpose of this gathering."

Hank stood to face the officer. "There are no rules about sitting around a campfire talking."

"I shall check into that. In the meantime, I suggest you men think hard about your duty to your country. I understand that I shall be heading a squad of Pennsylvania Militiamen. In the event that any of you privates are under my command, here is some advice. Quite plainly, I hate the British. I am here to win independence for the colonies. I will not stop short of that goal!

"I wouldn't want to think you fellows were considering desertion—or worse. For I will tolerate *nothing* but total patriotism. Do you understand?"

Hank remained standing but did not speak. He wanted to laugh. What a lot of hot air for a simple corporal, the lowest-ranking officer! Every man around this campfire knew more about war than this dandy.

"You," the corporal pointed his well-made bayonet at Hank. "Your name and rank."

"Private Hank Roberts," Hank said. Then he added, "Sir."

The corporal slowly lowered his bayonet. A strange look crossed his face. For a minute, he looked confused, then almost friendly.

The new officer nodded and seemed to have forgotten his thoughts. He turned his horse. Then, pulling himself together, he said, "Good morning men. In the future I suggest you use the night hours for sleep."

Then, before spurring his horse toward camp, the new corporal looked closely at Hank again. He shook his head, and muttering to himself, rode away.

Family Business

Hank, Ike, and the other men hurried back to their cabins. It was nearly sunrise. For a long time the men lay on their bunks in silence. Finally Ike got up to stoke the fire.

Wallace asked, "Do you think he will report us to Captain Alexander?"

"What were we doing wrong?" Dorian demanded.

No one replied. They all knew the answer. If reported, a secret gathering in the middle of the night would bring punishment. The real question was how many lashings . . . or would it be a bullet?

"He only has Hank's name, anyway," Dorian smiled wickedly.

"Don't worry about that," Hank answered. "No one would forget your face."

Ike laughed loudly.

"Shut up," Dorian snarled.

"Didn't you hear what the southerner said?" asked Hank. "He said he was a new corporal in Captain Alexander's company. He said he was to head up a squad of Pennsylvania Militiamen. . . ."

Hank was interrupted by a loud banging on the door. "Open up!" someone shouted. Dorian threw himself on his bunk and began to fake sleep. Hank opened the door.

"Privates!" Captain Alexander strode inside stepping high as if to show off his fancy knee-high boots. Those that could, jumped to their feet and saluted. "Meet your new corporal."

Walking in the door behind the captain was the southern stranger, as Hank suspected. The new corporal saluted the men. Then he shot an angry glance at one man who had not risen from his bunk.

"What's that man doing—?" the corporal demanded, but he cut himself off. The man who didn't rise was soaked in sweat, though the room was freezing cold. His red-rimmed eyes looked like empty sockets inside his bony face.

"Camp fever," Hank said.

The new corporal cleared his throat and turned away. Hank shook his head. This man had a lot to learn. He would see many sights worse than this before the week was out.

Then Captain Alexander spoke up in his deep voice. "Men, I expect you to obey the corporal's every order." With that, the captain left.

So, thought Hank, the corporal must not have told the captain about the meeting. The whole cabin remained standing and silent as the corporal stepped up to Hank. Their noses were inches apart.

"We meet again," the corporal said. He tapped the butt of his musket on the dirt floor. "Step outside with me, Private Roberts."

Hank followed the corporal. His back prickled with pain at the thought of lashings. Many times he'd seen privates lashed until their backs were ribboned with cuts.

But when Hank faced the corporal outside, the man looked almost friendly. Standing in the snow, the corporal said, "Tell me about your little meeting a few hours ago."

"There's nothing to tell," Hank replied.

"No?" The corporal drew up a frown. "You can't fool me, Private. I could smell you mutineers a mile away. Even if I hadn't overheard your talk."

Hank knew the man was bluffing. He hadn't overheard a thing. If he had, he would have known that Hank argued in support of Washington.

"Imagine what a fine start I could make in my army career," the corporal went on. "I simply have to inform Captain Alexander that I've discovered a ring of mutineers. You know that Captain Alexander is a fine and fiery patriot. Surely I'd be promoted right away."

Hank remained silent.

"However, Private, I am not interested in getting any of Washington's few troops in trouble. No, I will not give the British that victory. We need every able-bodied soldier we can get. I too am a patriot, and my career comes second to that.

"As I told you last night, independence and nothing less is my goal. Until the day the British are gone from this continent, I shall not rest."

Very noble, thought Hank. And very easy to say on a full stomach.

A bitter wind rushed by. Hank shivered, his very bones feeling like ice. The corporal pulled his fur collar in around his neck. Then he leaned forward.

"You seem like a reasonable man, Private Roberts. I hope to enlist your help. You see, I know quite a lot about you." The corporal paused and smiled. Hank knew he was trying to scare him. So Hank worked hard to keep his face blank. He would not take any bait from this conceited southern fellow.

"Let's see," the corporal said, as he began pacing in the snow. "Your father was a shoemaker from Stonesbury, Massachusetts. You refused to follow in his business, choosing instead to become a farmer. Your cousin,

Nathan, took your place in your father's shop. I understand you are bitter about this arrangement." The corporal smiled.

Hank stared at the new officer. He was unable now to hide his complete shock. How did the man know all this.

"You see," continued the man in his strong southern accent. "I was most disappointed to find my own cousin attending secret and rebellious meetings in the woods."

"Cousin—?"

"My name is Samuel Dunford from South Carolina. Your father was my mother's brother, and not a very fond one at that."

Hank remained speechless.

Dunford went on. "Your father offered my father three cows as a dowry for my mother. Needless to say, Father laughed in his face. Oh, he never got over that one." Dunford threw back his head and laughed as if he owned the world.

Now Hank was furious. He'd certainly had his differences with his father. But he would not have him laughed at by a fancily dressed southerner. Hank said, "Yes, and from what I understand your father was little more than a pirate. He left you and your mother to your own resources."

"It's true," Dunford said plainly. "And I can tell you my mother's resources were plenty. She did very well for herself in South Carolina. Thank goodness she didn't stay in this cold, gray country."

"Well you are such a *strong* patriot," Hank replied. "Then you know that most of our great thinkers are from New England—'this cold, gray country,' as you call it."

"Perhaps," smiled Dunford, enjoying the game. "But the greatest leader of all is a southerner, George Washington."

Hank did not reply. Then Dunford said, "In any case, I have decided not to turn you in."

"Because we are family?"

"Because I know that no grandson of Samuel Roberts could be all bad. He was a fine man, my mother tells me. I am named for him, of course."

"Spare me your good deeds. Turn me in if you wish. For I am not to be tested or shamed into 'good behavior.' I shall continue doing as my conscience bids."

"And what is it that your conscience bids?" Dunford asked.

"To do anything I can to save the lives of as many men here as possible."

"Do you not think that's what General Washington and the others have in mind?"

"What they have in mind means little to me right now. So far, all I've seen are death and suffering."

Dunford puffed up his chest. "Independence, Hank, independence! Don't you understand what we are about?"

"What does independence mean to a starving man?" Hank stepped closer to Dunford. "I am not unfamiliar with your cause, Corporal Dunford. I am in support of it. But I cannot look at the sick, dying men of this camp and talk about great ideas."

"You needn't worry so," the corporal said lightly. "The salmon will be running in the river soon, I understand. Then the men shall eat."

"Thousands of men have already died! Thousands! You've been here just one morning. You've no idea what you're talking about! Walk through camp and take a look at the graves. Look at the men with missing limbs. Listen to the screams from the hospital. See what this camp at Valley Forge is really like."

Dunford's face turned dark. "I cannot allow our family connection to permit you to speak to an officer that way. You are addressing your corporal!"

"No. Right now I am speaking to my cousin, and little more." Hank turned and began marching back to the cabin.

"Private Roberts!"

Hank turned and met his cousin's eyes. He thought that Corporal Dunford would do very well under Captain Alexander. Grand ideas, these men had. Ike was absolutely right about there being two kinds of patriots. Oh, these men could carry on for hours about great lofty causes. But who was fighting, starving, dying? Not the officers. Not the Continental Congress. Who were they to say whether a simple soldier was a true patriot or not?

Dunford's face softened. "We needn't be enemies, you know. We *are* fighting on the same side."

"That is not entirely clear to me," Hank said. "It seems to me that you put hatred of the British above love for Americans. Perhaps I will think about hating the British some day. But for now, my concerns are the sick and starving countrymen under my nose."

With that, Hank turned on his heels and left Corporal Dunford standing in the snow.

The Trip to the Farmhouse

For the next several days Corporal Dunford gave orders right and left. Hank felt a bitter anger mounting in his chest. The new officer wanted bigger woodpiles. He wanted his sentries to pace rather than sit by a warm fire. He expected his squad to stand each time he entered the cabin.

The men tried to follow his orders. But they were weak, cold, and hungry. By the week's end four men in the squad had dropped to the ground from exhaustion. Then Corporal Dunford finally seemed to see the truth. He realized that his men had barely enough strength to survive.

Hank wondered how Corporal Dunford couldn't see that he was driving the men toward mutiny. The secret meetings continued. But so far, the soldiers' constant disagreeing kept them from taking any action.

Hank knew he had to do *something* to calm his own despair. Something that might help the men and keep them from causing more hardship for themselves.

A week after Corporal Dunford's arrival, Hank put his plan into action. He waited until he was pretty sure the other men in his cabin were asleep. Then he rolled off his bunk, quietly lifted his musket, and slipped out the door.

Two sentries sat sleeping by a dying campfire. Hank didn't want to risk getting a bullet in his back. So he crept up to one of the men and tapped him on the shoulder. Both sentries jumped awake. Their eyes bounced about with fright. Hank might have been a superior officer.

Hank squatted and whispered something to one of the sentries. He looked over his shoulder and then whispered to the other man. The second man shrugged and nodded. Hank ran quickly toward the woods.

A full moon and the brightness of the fallen snow made the going easy. In spite of his leg, Hank was able to move quickly.

As he reached the edge of the forest, Hank suddenly heard footsteps padding after him. Had the sentries changed their minds? He turned, expecting to face a musket. Instead he saw Ike hurrying to catch up with him.

"What are you doing?" Hank whispered.

"I knew you planned to leave," said the boy. "Tonight I saw you wrap your feet carefully. I saw you place your musket by your bed. I knew you planned on walking somewhere."

Hank shook his head. Only Ike would notice such things. "But why did you follow?"

"I thought you might run away. So I would go, too. You have looked out for me in camp. Without you, Dorian and the others might tear me apart."

Hank nodded. "But I'm not running away. I'm going to my old farm, eight miles from here. I'm hoping when the redcoats raided the place, they missed a second cellar I have in the barn. I had many potatoes there. Perhaps they haven't rotted. I thought the men in our cabin at least . . . it was something I could do. I figure if I hurry I can get there and back before the light of morning."

"Your leg," Ike said simply.

"Yes, it hurts. But a little food might go a long way toward calming the men."

"You don't want to see a rebellion, do you?" Ike asked.

"I'm afraid no one would be helped."

"I saw you whisper to the sentries," Ike said. "So I said I was with you. What did you tell them?"

Hank smiled. "I caught them sleeping. I told them their commanding officer wouldn't like to hear that. Then I promised them potatoes for their fire before dawn."

Ike smiled and fell in step beside Hank. The man and boy walked in silence most of the way. When they reached the clearing where Hank's house stood, Hank reached out and stopped Ike. Two horses were tied up outside the house.

"Someone must be inside," Hank whispered. "In *my* house," he added snarling.

Slowly Hank and Ike crept up to the house. They crouched below the window, then eased their heads up to look inside. There they saw dozens of bags of wheat, flour, corn meal, and potatoes. Cabbages and carrots, too, were piled up on the floor.

"A British stockpile?" whispered Ike.

Hank's stomach growled at the sight of the food.

"Careful," Ike warned. "Look for guards."

But Hank's mind deserted him. His churning stomach took over. "Come on," he said too loudly. "Let's gather as much food as we can. If we're careful, we can come back another night. With this much food, they won't miss what we can carry."

Hank stood up and began walking toward the front of the house. "Wait," warned Ike. But it was too late.

From around the side of the house came two redcoats carrying muskets.

"What's this?" said one in a husky German accent. He was tall and thin, and he wore a long, droopy mustache.

The other, a short stocky man, shoved his musket toward Hank and Ike. He too spoke with a German accent when he ordered, "Drop your muskets. Then get inside."

Hessians, thought Hank. These were the German soldiers paid by the British to fight. He was too angry to be frightened. These men had a lot of nerve using his house as freely as if they owned it.

Held at gunpoint, Hank and Ike marched toward the farmhouse. The Hessians spoke to each other in rapid German. Hank thought they sounded very angry with each other. They were so busy arguing they didn't see Ike make his move.

Just as they reached the door, Ike lunged to the side. He ran so fast that Hank saw only a streak. The two Germans stood blinking for a second before they realized what was happening.

"Come back," shouted the stocky one.

"You fool," said the other guard. "You think he will come just by calling him."

As the guards began to argue again in German, Ike jumped upon one of their horses. In a split second, he slashed the rope that tied the horse to a tree.

Finally one Hessian lifted his musket and fired. The horse reared up and bucked. Its legs buckled and it fell to the ground. The next shot got Ike in the arm as he fell off the horse. The boy got to his feet as quickly as he could and began to run.

The two redcoats looked at each other. "Go get him," said one.

"*You* go get him," said the other.

"I hit him. He will fall and die on his own."

"That was *my* shot that hit him. Besides, what if he doesn't die?"

"It's just an Indian *boy*. Let him go."

A Turncoat Discovered

"You!" The short, stocky soldier jabbed Hank with his musket. "Get in the house."

"What are we going to tell the general?" the thin man asked when they had gone inside.

"What should we tell him? That we were sleeping? That we almost let this sneaky rebel steal some food? Don't be stupid! We don't tell him anything. After he leaves, we'll get rid of this one."

"I guess you are right. We will have to kill him. After all, we can't tell the general. And we can't send him on his way. But how do we do it? And what do we do with the body?"

"Idiot!" cried the other. Then they began arguing again. Hank tried to breathe evenly. He began to think that Ike's daring move wasn't so foolish. He'd rather bleed to death in the forest than die at the hands of these men.

Suddenly Hank heard a galloping sound outside. "It's the captain!" one of the guards whispered. "Quick, put him somewhere."

The two Hessians ran about in circles for ten seconds before they could decide what to do. They looked like confused chickens. If his life hadn't been in danger, Hank would have laughed.

Finally one of the men pushed him up the ladder into the loft. He said, "You stay completely quiet. One word and we kill you, understand?"

"Quite clearly," Hank said.

"Not a sound," the other guard added. The two soldiers rushed out to greet the captain.

Hank wondered where Ike was. Probably bleeding to death in the snow somewhere. He should have ordered the boy back to the cabin.

How foolish he'd been to let Ike risk punishment for desertion. We are all becoming monsters and madmen, he thought.

The door opened and Hank heard three men enter the house. Then a deep voice asked, "Has General Rothchild arrived yet?"

"No sir," answered one of the Hessians.

"Ah, he is always late," said the deep voice. It sounded strangely familiar to Hank.

"Yes sir," answered the Hessian.

Hank slid on his belly across the floor until he could see down into the kitchen. He had a good view of the newcomer and the two Hessians. Hank almost cried out loud at the sight of the man with the deep voice.

There, pacing in Hank's own kitchen, was Captain Alexander of the Continental Army. For a moment Hank felt delight. All this had been a big mistake. Certainly if the Hessians took orders from Captain Alexander, they sided with the patriots! Hank need only show himself to the captain. He began to move toward the loft ladder. Then something occurred to him.

It didn't make sense that the Hessians would help a patriot captain. Besides, if Captain Alexander knew about all this food, how come he hadn't had it delivered to Valley Forge?

The truth suddenly hit Hank with the force of a blow to the head. The outspoken, so-called "patriot" was a turncoat!

Seconds later a British officer came through the kitchen door. "General Rothchild," said Captain Alexander, taking the British man's hand.

A cold chill shook Hank's very bones.

Rothchild asked, "Do you have any information for us?"

Alexander smiled a sly smile. "A small caravan of food for the Continental Army should be arriving next week. Keep the road well guarded, and you will easily overtake it.

"However, General Howe in Philadelphia needn't worry," the captain went on. "The rebels at Valley Forge are barely alive."

Hank couldn't believe his eyes when Captain Alexander actually laughed. "Washington is quite a joke. He's got a new German fellow, named Von Steuben, drilling soldiers. As if they'll have the strength to march out of there in the spring! That man just won't give up."

"Any trouble here?" Rothchild asked the Hessians.

"No sir."

"No strangers sniffing around, no local colonists asking questions?"

"No sir. All's been quiet. Not a single person."

"Good," said Rothchild. Then he passed a sack of gold to Alexander. "Keep up the good work. And I shall see you next week."

Captain Alexander and General Rothchild left at the same time. Hank listened to the hooves of their horses. His mind seemed to work in slow motion as the truth sunk in. Once a week Captain Alexander left camp for a meeting here. For sacks of gold, he helped the British cut off wagons full of good food headed for Valley Forge. And he laughed about the starving patriots! Worst of all,

Hank was afraid that he would never live to report this.

As soon as the officers were out of ear-shot, the Hessians began their usual arguing. Hank crawled over to the top of the loft ladder. The two Germans were directly below him. They had begun pushing one another in anger.

Hank took a deep breath. Then he leapt down from the loft. He let loose a blood-curdling scream as he landed on top of the two men. They crumbled beneath him, breaking his fall.

Hank jumped to his feet and made for the door. His only hope was that he could get out before the men recovered. As he grabbed the doorknob, the sound of musket fire rang out.

It took Hank a few seconds to realize he hadn't been hit. He couldn't believe it. The shot had blown a hole through the door a foot away. Were these men bad shots! He was only ten feet away from them.

"Stupid!" shouted the tall guard. "If you kill him here, how do we explain the pool of blood?" Still, Hank didn't dare move. The Hessians pinned him to the door with muskets.

"Trying to play tricks with us, are you?" the other guard asked. "We cannot afford to keep you around any longer. What is your last wish?"

"Quaint idea, a last wish," Hank said sarcastically.

"What is 'quaint'?" one asked.

Hank knew he needed time. He was sure he could outsmart these two. So he explained the word 'quaint.' "It means sweet and old-fashioned. But I do have a last wish. I am a starving man. You have so much food here. Surely you can spare me one meal before I die. That is all I ask, to die with a full stomach."

"That can't hurt," one guard said, shrugging his shoulders. "What do you want?"

"Do you have any meat?"

"Ha! The man wants meat?" the stocky guard said.

"You ask him what he wants, what do you expect him to say? Of course he wants meat!"

"I suppose next he'll want his potatoes cooked."

"That would be nice, please," Hank said. The truth was, with his death close at hand, Hank had lost his appetite. But he felt that these two guards were fools. If he could stall for time, maybe he could outsmart them.

The two guards held their muskets on Hank while he put the potatoes on the fire. Then the three men sat in complete silence until they were done. Each man ate two potatoes and some dried meat.

Then the short, stocky guard said, "Now it's time."

"Outside," said the other. "Where we can cover up the blood. Come on, *march*."

Hank went first. The two guards followed with their muskets trained on his head. Outside a beautiful morning was dawning. The sun was actually coming out for the first time in weeks. Snow dripped and melted off the trees. Hank thought the little warmth from the sun was the best gift he could have before dying.

"What's that?" the short German asked.

Hank listened and he heard something too. It sounded like many horses galloping through the woods.

"Quick," said the other guard. "Get him back in the house."

"No," said the first one. "We must shoot him now."

Two muskets were placed against Hank's head. He closed his eyes. The last thing he wanted to remember was the warmth of the sun on his back. Then he waited for the blackness of death to fall upon him.

A *Traitor* Exposed

"Put down your muskets or we shoot!" came a voice from the trees. Hank opened his eyes to see the two Hessians dropping their muskets.

Five men on horseback came out of the woods. Corporal Samuel Dunford led the soldiers. On a horse next to him rode Wallace with Ike in front of him. The boy held one hand clamped to his arm, below a tight tourniquet. His shirt was stained with blood.

Hank felt faint. He had to shake his head hard to keep from passing out.

"Close in, men," Dunford ordered. "Wallace, strip the two Germans of their guns. When we leave, you're in charge of taking them back to camp. Parker and Thomson, you two will stay to guard the house until someone returns for you."

As Wallace tied up the Hessians, Hank just looked up at the sky. He stamped the earth beneath his feet. He turned his face to the breeze. He was *alive*.

For a moment Hank felt nothing but joy. Then he thought of the next problem waiting for him. He walked slowly to meet Dunford. "Morning Corporal. Guess it doesn't matter much whether they shoot me or you do. I suppose you think I was deserting, though I swear to you I was not. But before you do anything, you should know that that house is full of food."

"Yes, Ike told me." Dunford looked angry. "But you went against orders coming out here."

"Yes, I know. But it turned out well."

"Tell that to Captain Alexander! He was quite busy this morning. But I am sure he shall learn somehow that I took three horses to rescue you."

"Maybe you should know—" Hank began.

Dunford swung off his horse. "That's three horses belonging to *officers*, Private."

Hank looked at the ground. There were very few horses still alive at Valley Forge. Even fewer were strong enough to ride any distance. But Hank knew he had to make Dunford realize his efforts were far from wasted. "Corporal Dunford—" Hank began again.

But Dunford ignored him. He started shouting orders to the men again. "Ike, you ride back with Private Roberts and me. You need to get to the hospital."

Hank climbed onto the same horse as Ike and took the reins. The Hessians followed on their horses. Wallace rode in back, a musket pointed at the Hessians.

"Don't try anything," Hank warned the captured men with a wink. "Wallace is a much better shot than you are."

Then Hank said to Ike, "Why didn't you just give the corporal directions? You're going to bleed to death."

"White men don't understand fifty paces past a stand of sugar pine. I was afraid they would not find you in time."

"He insisted on showing the way," Dunford said, still growling with anger. "Though I must say your rescue hardly seems worth the effort of five men and horses."

"I'm touched by your concern for family," Hank said. "What about the food? Will that make my life worthwhile?"

Anger set a hard line across Dunford's mouth. Hank knew the corporal had risked his entire career for him. The few good horses in camp were kept for emergencies and high officers. Dunford must have nearly stolen them.

"Well, you made a good decision in my case," Hank said. "I have gathered some very important information for the Continental Army."

Corporal Dunford did not look interested. So Hank said, "Sir, you may find this very hard to believe. But I know for a fact that Captain Alexander is a traitor and a spy."

Now Corporal Dunford swung around on his horse. "Why you sneaky little lying mutineer! I never dreamed you'd stoop so low as to—"

"Cousin, believe me and listen. No grandson of Samuel Roberts would lie."

Corporal Dunford pulled in the corners of his mouth. His skin was ashen. Hank saw that his hands holding the reins were shaking. In a thin voice, Dunford said, "Go on. Why do you say this?"

Hank explained why he had left camp to go to the farmhouse. He told Dunford the whole story of what had happened while he was there. The corporal did not speak a word, though Hank could see that he listened closely.

"You can believe me or not," Hank said. "I only ask for one thing. Please give me a full hearing in the presence of General Washington."

"Ha!" Dunford cried. His voice cracked as he said, "Washington would hardly believe a private's word against a captain's."

Dunford rubbed his brow. Then he fixed his eyes on Hank. "But I believe you. A grandson of Samuel Roberts would not lie."

Dunford smiled sadly. Hank could see how upset Dunford was to learn that the man he had admired was a traitor. Hank also knew that his cousin had risked his own neck for him. Dunford could be awfully harsh at times. But Hank now felt that underneath it all he was a good man.

By the time they had reached camp Dunford's sorrow had hardened. He spotted Captain Alexander at a distance. "There he is," Dunford said under his breath. "The dirty double-crossing dog. Follow me."

"Corporal Dunford," Hank cautioned. "Shouldn't we talk to someone else first?"

But Dunford spurred his horse to a gallop. Hank tried to keep up the pace, but was slowed by his concern for Ike's wounds. Taking up the rear were the two Hessians with Wallace guarding them.

Hank pulled up in time to see that Corporal Dunford did not salute the captain.

A mean frown creased Captain Alexander's face. His deep voice boomed as he demanded, "What are you dragging in here, Dunford? Why, that's an officer's horse these two privates are riding!"

Dunford said, "Never mind the horse. Tell me, do you recognize these two men."

Captain Alexander looked at the Hessians and his face drained of all color. In that moment, it was obvious to Dunford that Hank had spoken the complete truth.

But Captain Alexander stood a bit taller. He leveled his eyes at the Hessians and said, "I've never seen them in my life. And if you don't take these privates and get out—"

"Captain Alexander," Hank said. "I watched the whole thing from the loft of the farmhouse. The sack of gold? General Rothchild?"

Captain Alexander's lips started twitching. He looked quickly over his shoulder and then said to Dunford, "Look, Corporal. You and I can work this out. If I say the word, you'll be promoted to a sergeant. The private could be . . ."

"What about Ike?" Hank asked harshly. The captain looked at the young Indian boy slumped in front of Hank. "He saved my life, and in doing so uncovered a spy. Why, I think he should have your job, Captain."

Now the captain's face turned almost purple. "You know, I could have all of you shot. All I'd have to tell Washington is that you were deserting. And horse-stealing! I could—"

"I don't think so, Captain. Let's go, Privates. Bring the Hessians." Dunford swung his horse around and Hank followed.

"I warn you," the turncoat captain hissed after them. "Washington will believe me before you any day. I'll have you shot for disloyalty."

Outside Washington's cabin, Dunford said, "Wait here."

"I'm going to take Ike to the hospital," Hank said. "Something has to be done about his wound."

Hank swung the horse around and headed toward the privates' quarters.

"Not the hospital," Ike whispered weakly.

Hank smiled. Ike was just following Hank's own advice. So Hank took Ike back to the cabin. There he stoked the fire and boiled some water. With a knife, Hank carved out the bullet. Then he cleaned and dressed the boy's wound.

"There you go, young man. Your arm is going to be all right."

But Ike had passed out into a deep sleep. He looked more boy than man now. Hank smiled at him and thought of his own children. He ruffled the boy's hair and said softly, "You saved my life, Ike."

A Small Feast

Hank slept the rest of that day and all that night. When he finally awoke, the cabin was empty. Hank crawled out of bed, wondering where Ike might be.

He threw open the cabin door and found the entire squad. They were telling jokes around a big outdoor campfire. A strong spring sun shone down like liquid gold on the men. At last, weather warm enough to let them come out of the smoky cabins!

Hank smiled broadly when he saw Ike. The men had built him an outdoor bunk. They had gathered together the few blankets the squad had. Ike was wrapped up and laid next to the campfire. The boy was sleeping. Hank realized it must be midmorning.

"There's Hank!" shouted Wallace. "Three cheers!" The men joined Wallace and sang out, "Three cheers!" "Three cheers!" Only Dorian sat silently, poking the fire with a stick.

"What's going on?" Hank asked, rubbing his eyes. The sun was bright!

Wallace explained. "All day yesterday the men made trips to your farmhouse. We carried back all the food. Today the generals are rationing it. We should have ours within the hour." The men laughed like children.

Hank swallowed hard. Sunshine, laughter, and food all in one day were almost too much to take. The men had even pulled together to make Ike comfortable. Maybe, just maybe, things would now take a turn for the better.

Hank looked out beyond his own cabin and squad. He saw several campfires dotting the huge camp. Men everywhere were celebrating the sunshine and the promised meal.

As the men waited for the food, they talked of home, friends, and past adventures. Hank noticed that no one grumbled about Valley Forge. No one mentioned rebellion.

Finally an officer dropped off a bundle of food. The men in Hank's squad voted him cook. There wasn't a lot of food for each man after it was divided up. But it was a lot more than they'd had in a long time.

Hank made a watery vegetable stew. He kept the meat aside, because he knew the men would want it plain. There was enough wheat flour for everyone to have several firecakes. This would be a small feast.

As they ate, the patriot soldiers became happier and happier. Even Dorian laughed at the jokes and listened quietly as the men spoke of America's independent future.

The tide had turned. Hank knew the sunshine was helping as much as the food. Still, he was glad he'd been able to help make a difference.

Hank kept a close watch on Ike all day. The boy was very weak from having lost so much blood. He drifted in and out of sleep. Every time he awoke, Hank tried to feed him a bit more.

Later in the afternoon, Hank unwrapped Ike's bandage to check the wound. It seemed to be all right. As he dressed the wound again, he heard a lot of noise behind him. Hank glanced over his shoulder, and saw the whole squad jump to its feet and salute.

Then Hank saw Corporal Dunford joining the men at the campfire. At his side stood General George Washington. Hank stood and saluted. Even Ike saluted from his bed of poles.

"Good afternoon, men. Privates Roberts and Ike?" Washington asked.

"Yes sir," Hank and Ike said at the same time.

Washington stepped forward and shook Hank's hand. "I wanted to thank you personally for the meal you provided for our troops.

"And you," Washington said, squatting beside Ike's bed and taking his hand. "You saved your friend's life. And in so doing, you uncovered a traitor in our ranks. Well done. When you are both well enough to move about, I'd like you to have supper with me in my quarters."

Washington stood and looked over Corporal Dunford's squad. "Good day men," he said and left.

Hank heard Dorian mutter, "Dinner! How do they rate?" But the rest of the men paid no attention. They all began talking at once about having the famous general at their own campfire.

Corporal Dunford strolled over to Hank's side and said quietly, "Well, you were lucky this time." Hank glared at the corporal, ready for an argument. But the officer's eyes were warm and friendly. "You made a foolish move in sneaking out of camp as you did. But I will say that, in the end, you did a great deed."

"I believe in taking care of the problems before my eyes, sir," Hank replied.

"I can understand that better now. I will admit I was a bit green when I first arrived here at Valley Forge. The problems are far worse than I thought. Now I can better appreciate your practical approach."

Hank smiled. "Thank you, Corporal Dunford."

The officer smiled too and took Hank by the shoulders. "To you," he said with a chuckle, "it's Cousin Sam."

Dunford left, and Hank looked up at the blue sky. This one meal would hardly pull the men through until spring. But it certainly had picked up their spirits.

Besides, riding back from the farmhouse, Hank had noticed a few tiny buds on the trees. Today, with the sun out, a few songbirds had broken the deathly silence of winter. Soon the salmon would be running up the river. Then they would leave this death hole called Valley Forge. And before long, the colonies would be free of British rule—forever.